CANDYCE
A Thai Street Dog's Tale

Written by Soleil McKirdy

Illustrations by Daryna Kaminska

CANDYCE
A Thai Street Dog's Tale

Thailand

Hello

My name is Candyce and this story is all about me.

I'm not just an ordinary old dog you see.

I was born on the streets of Bangkok, but it was not a good life for me.

I felt so scared, and I was always sick and hungry.

Then one day it started to rain. It poured and it poured and a big flood came.

The deep, muddy waters nearly swept me away, but Lek the elephant whisperer rescued me and took me home to stay.

And so Elephant Nature Park became my home, but something was missing, I still felt alone.

There were dogs, cats and elephants of course. A bear, some chickens and even a horse.

Monkeys, pigs and buffalo all live here too.

All kinds of animals everywhere, but it is definitely not a zoo!

I had food and friends, but I still felt so lonely.

Life in a sanctuary sure beats the streets, but it isn't quite homely.

Then one day out of the blue I met a new human who promised that I'd be adopted too.

So now I had my own Mum, but I would have to wait for the day she would come back for me.
It was a very distant date.

I waited and I waited and I waited some more. I waited so long that my hope was all gone and my heart sank to the floor.

All my friends left me for their amazing new lives, but I was still waiting, it didn't seem right.

Two years went by then it was finally my turn. I didn't know where I was going, but I would soon learn.

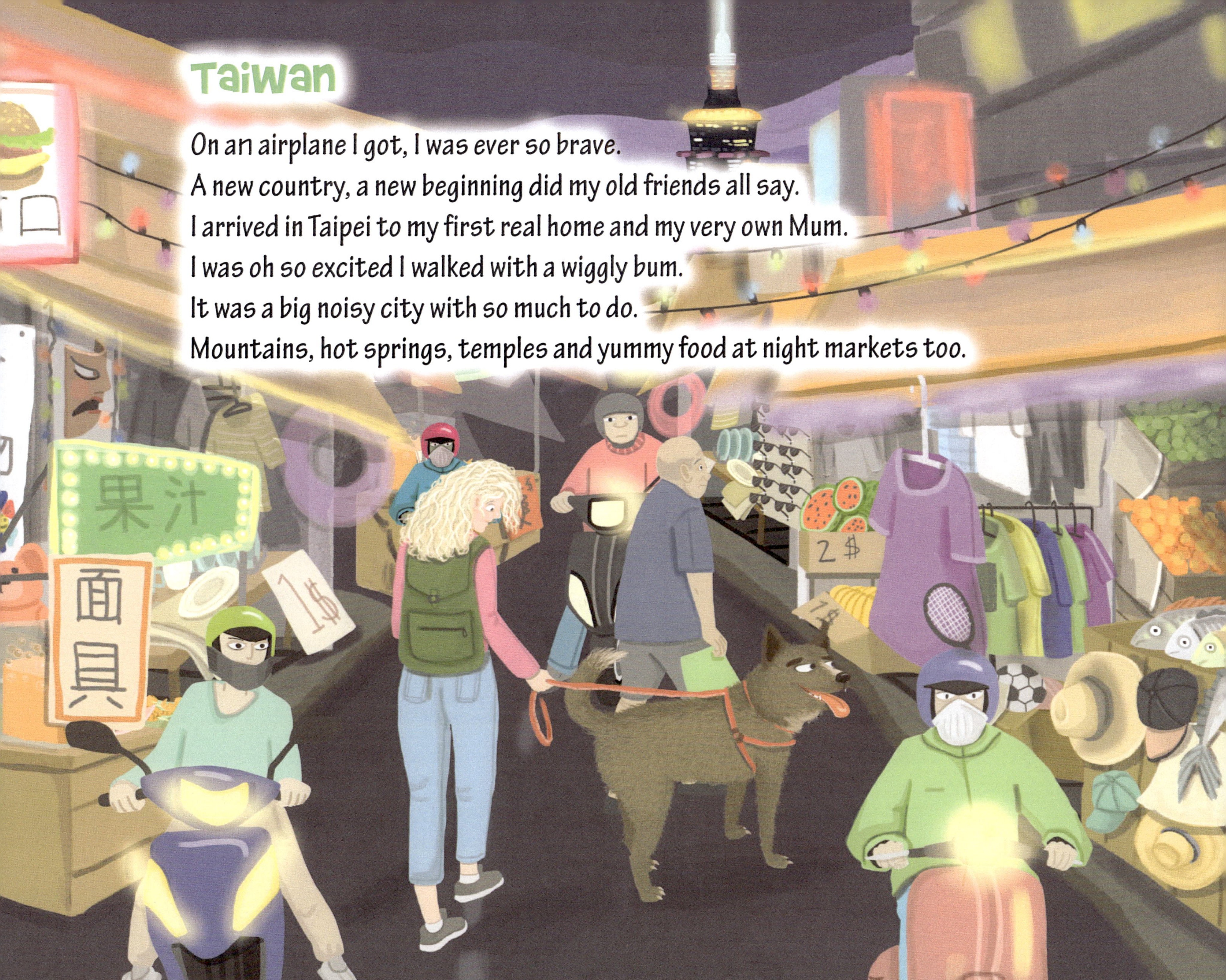

Taiwan

On an airplane I got, I was ever so brave.
A new country, a new beginning did my old friends all say.
I arrived in Taipei to my first real home and my very own Mum.
I was oh so excited I walked with a wiggly bum.
It was a big noisy city with so much to do.
Mountains, hot springs, temples and yummy food at night markets too.

果汁

面具

1$

2 $

1$

Before I knew it my time in Taiwan had come to an end.

Another flight, more adventures and hopefully some new friends.

I leapt off the plane and I jumped in the car. I drove through San Franscisco, then Hollywood, I felt like a movie star!

I saw giant trees, wildflowers and so many squirrels. I was oh so happy I pranced around with a bum full of jiggles.

In San Diego I arrived on a hot summer's day, so I headed to the beach for a splash and a play.
I chased and chased and chased my new dog friends some more, then I splashed in the water.
I had such a ball!

Czech Republic

Another day, another flight, I was getting used to this adventurous life.

I was so excited to get there, but when I landed the ground was so cold and white!

I walked around Prague for hours that day.

There were so many amazing places that I wished I could stay.

I explored old buildings and cobble stone streets. I pranced around parks and ancient castles until I had cold and frozen feet.

Germany

Once again it was time to leave.

The train sped from Prague station with a big snort and a heave.

"Off to Berlin" my Mum told me. "A big, fun city with so much to see".

I walked past high walls with big statues and busy cafes on wide streets. The air filled with the smells of delicious food I was not allowed to eat.

Next stop a country full of bicycles and flowers, and so many windmills that look like tall towers.

Do you think you might know which country it is?

NETHERLANDS

It's the Netherlands!

Amsterdam: I like it here. Canals and bicycles everywhere and the weather was clear.

The bus took me to this most amazing place. I'd never seen anything like it. What a blissful space!

Fields of colourful tulips that stretched as far as the eye could see. So many people asked to take my photo and said that I am beautiful and as well-behaved as could be.

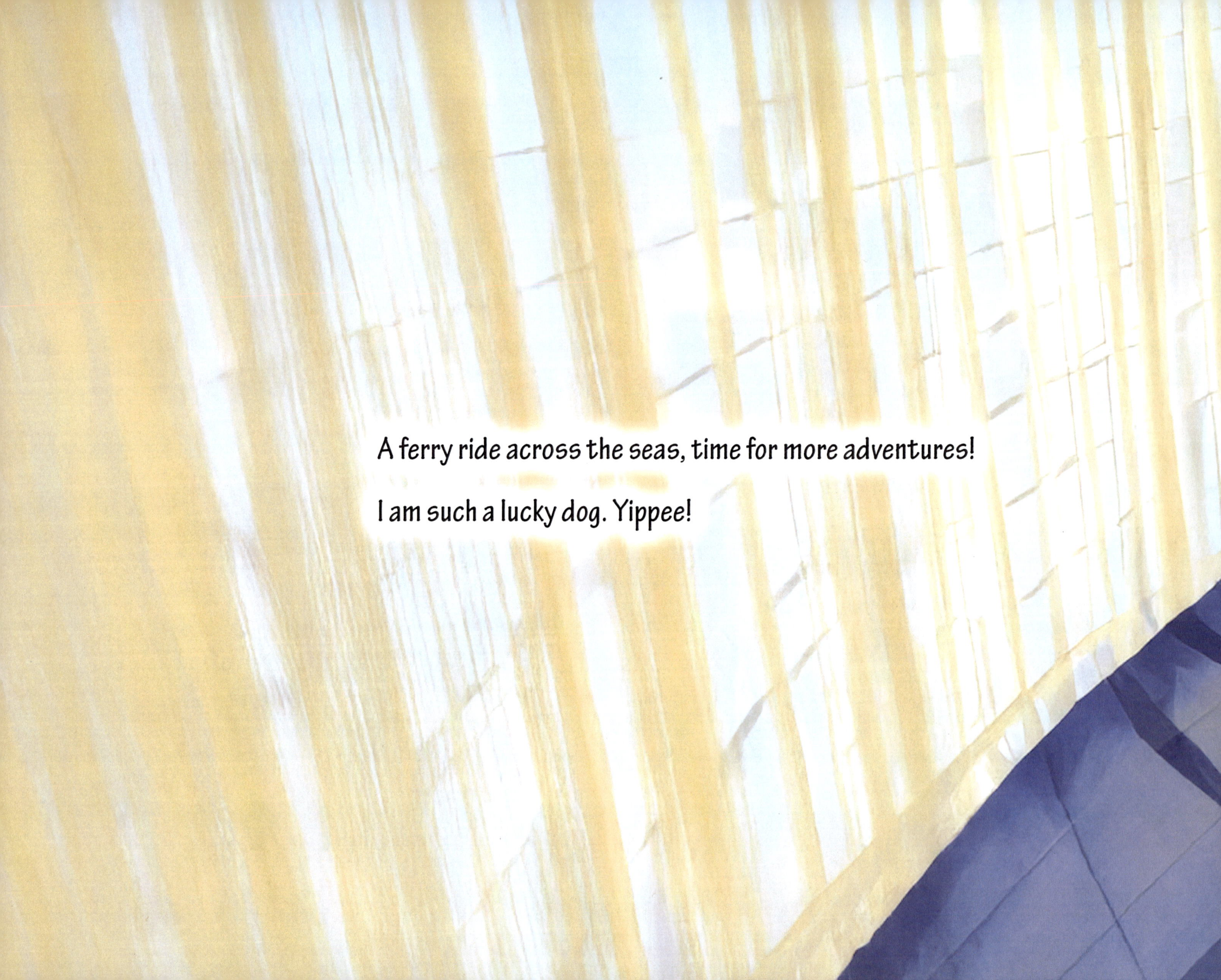

A ferry ride across the seas, time for more adventures!

I am such a lucky dog. Yippee!

From north to south, east to west, these things in the UK are what I liked best.

I went on the tube and I rode a big red bus.
I chased squirrels in the park for hours and I even met some other rescued street dogs. Woof!

From London to York and Edinburgh too, Bristol and Liverpool; there was so much to see and do.

I met some famous people; I saw many amazing things, like The Beatles, Buckingham Palace and the Forest of Dean.

But like all great things, they must come to an end.
Farewell Great Britain and so long to all my new friends.

New Zealand

The big day came; we were on the move once again.

Life seems like an adventure that will never ever end.

I waited and I waited, and I waited some more.

It was such a long flight, oh what a bore!

To the far Deep South I would go; a place called Dunedin. The land of freezing cold winds, sheep and mountains capped in snow.

ultoo

Mum took me for amazing walks through forests of pine, but the lack of hot sun- that's where I draw the line!

I chased bunnies in the fields, I did zoomies on the beach, but all I really craved was the hot summer heat.

Just when I thought I'd be cold forever, an incredible thing happened that made me more excited than ever.

Do you know what happened next?

Come on, have a guess.

AUSTRALIA

AUSTRALIA!! I am coming your way.

The big southern land that I heard has so many sunny days.

Little did I know it when at the airport I arrived. Waiting for me was the most amazing, INCREDIBLE, TERRIFIC SURPRISE!

What!!? No crate in the cargo hold? Ooh this is the life!

I got the V.I.P treatment; my very own seat on a special doggy flight.

Finally, I have made it!

Australia I am here!

This little Thai dog has waited so many long years.

This travelling life has been so much fun, but now I'm in Australia I'm content to just laze around in the sun.

I have seen so many amazing places, the whole world I got to roam, but now Australia really is the place that I call home.

My name is Candyce and this is my story.

I have lived quite the life full of despair, pain and glory.

I've gone on lots of adventures, and I have travelled across the seas. But I will never forget where I came from, that little Bangkok street dog is still within me.

THE END

Thank you very much for reading😊

Candyce's Instagram is travelling_thai_dog if you would like to see
more photos from her amazing life and adventures.

Candyce started out life as a stray on the streets of Bangkok, Thailand. In 2011 a major flood took the life of many animals and people and left a trail of disease and destruction in its wake. Many street dogs that survived the initial flooding either succumbed to disease or starvation. Many others were captured and sold to the lucrative dog meat trade by people pretending to be rescuers. When Lek Chailert, the founder of Elephant Nature Park heard of their plight she and her team rescued several thousand dogs including Candyce and took several hundred of them back to Elephant Nature Park sanctuary near Chiang Mai. Although they were not setup to house or care for this sudden large influx of dogs; with the assistance of volunteers and donations they were able to swiftly build a dog sanctuary to accommodate the rescued dogs and provide them with basic veterinary care and food. My first visit and volunteer trip to the park was during this time and much of my visit was spent assisting with the building and setting up of the dog sanctuary area. Little did I know that a dog that would profoundly change my life was amongst them.

I first met Candyce (then named Pee Dee) whilst volunteering at Elephant Nature Park in December 2014. Although I had never considered having a dog before, it was love at first sight. Two years later I was finally able to adopt her after finishing my studies in Australia and then relocating to Taiwan (a category 3 country) with the plan to take her back to Australia with me after a year or two.

However, just two days before our scheduled flight to Australia, fate intervened when Candyce failed one of the mandatory blood tests required for Australian entry. This meant she would not be allowed to travel.

Vowing to never give up on my adoption promise to love and care for her for the rest of her life, I decided to do whatever it took to keep Candyce with me and to persevere with our dream of getting her home to Australia no matter how long it took. Doing whatever I had to do to achieve this, I applied for every job and scholarship I could find in any country where I could obtain a visa to stay and where Candyce would be able to travel. Eventually I was successful in securing a short-term teaching job in the Czech Republic, which enabled sufficient time to prepare Candyce for our onward journey to New Zealand where I was to take up the offer of a scholarship to study a master's degree.

In 2023 after 4 ½ years in New Zealand dog import requirements into Australia were changed, finally allowing Candyce to enter. She arrived in Australia in December 2023; her 11th country at the age of 12.5 years old. While I thought Candyce's story would end there, just 4 months after she landed in Australia, she was diagnosed with a large Peripheral Nerve Sheath tumour after suddenly developing a severe limp. The vet gave Candyce just weeks to live due to the severe pain she was experiencing from the tumour which was pressing on her spinal cord and impairing nerve function throughout her body. Despite this life-threatening health issue, Candyce continued to defy the odds and demonstrate that with determination, courage and perseverance anything was possible. She continued to live each day of her life to the fullest until the very end. Candyce passed away of kidney failure in June 2024. She was 13 years old.